Mabel Squirrel dug deep into the leaves. "I never thought this could be so much fun," she said.

"Good for your lungs, too," said the Cinnamon Hen.

Red and gold leaves swirled around them.

But the Cinnamon Hen seemed to be having such a
good time, racing along the hedge, laughing at the wind
and the way another prong sprung off her rake when she
hit a tree root, that Mabel Squirrel stood up and said,
"Wait! You can't do all that work by yourself."

"Work?" said the Cinnamon Hen. "This isn't work."

"Whatever it is," said Mabel, "I want to do it, too."

"Then get your rake," said the Cinnamon Hen.

"You're very strange today," said Mabel Squirrel.

"It's Autumn," said the Cinnamon Hen, as if that explained everything.

"Well," said Mabel, "if you insist." And she sat down on her step and watched.

"And the way the wind scatters the leaves just as soon as I get them into a pile."

"You do?" Mabel Squirrel studied her friend
thoughtfully.

"And the crunch," the Cinnamon Hen added, twisting
the toe of her galosh.

"Yes?" said Mabel. "Yes? Hm."

"I like the dust," said the Cinnamon Hen, taking a deep breath.

"I'd be happy to rake your leaves," said the Cinnamon Hen.

"Rake my leaves!" said Mabel. "You don't have to do that. I'll get to it. Eventually."

"No, no. I'll do it now," said the Cinnamon Hen.

"But why?" asked Mabel.

The Cinnamon Hen put on her red sweater, her black rubber galoshes, and, taking her rake with the two prongs missing, climbed the fence (though she'd always, until now, gone around it), and walked up to Mabel's door.

And as for pneumonia—well, she thought, last year I didn't get it. Why should I get it this year?

Then she looked over at Mabel Squirrel's yard.

It was still filled with leaves.

and stomping on them to make room for more,

and carrying the bags to the curb. Yes, she missed it.

She realized how much she missed the wonderful crackle,

and bending over to push the leaves into the bag,

But as soon as Mr. Rabbit drove off, the Cinnamon Hen looked sadly at her black rubber galoshes and the red sweater she wore every year when she raked leaves.

LEAVE THE RAKING
RABBIT'S
YARD
SERVICE
TO ME!

The Cinnamon Hen could see that Mr. Rabbit had lettered exactly those words on the pocket of his jacket.

"Rhubarb," said Mr. Rabbit. "Leave the Raking to Me," he added with a salute.

"I'll bet it would have taken *you* a lot longer," he said, when he came up to the door.

"Three hours," the Cinnamon Hen confessed, "and sometimes more."

"Just think," said Mr. Rabbit, "you don't have to worry about these leaves now."

"No," said the Cinnamon Hen, as she counted out the three-fifty.

"And you don't have to worry about pneumonia, bronchitis, or asthma."

"No, I guess not."

"And you get to rest."

"Yes," said the Cinnamon Hen, though she'd been longing the entire time to get out and rake leaves with Mr. Rabbit. "I suppose I could make a pie."

Then he brought out bags and packed the leaves in.
He even had a special barrel that held the bags. He was
finished with the yard in thirty minutes flat.

She went inside, made herself a cup of tea, and sat by the window.

Mr. Rabbit was a professional. He piled the leaves up with a blower.

"That's right," said Mr. Rabbit, already taking his
equipment out of the truck. "The dust is bad for your
lungs, too. You might start to cough and then you might
get asthma."

"I suppose you're right," said the Cinnamon Hen,
though she'd never thought much about asthma before.
Nor, for that matter, bronchitis or pneumonia.

"I don't mind," said the Cinnamon Hen.

"Don't mind?" said Mr. Rabbit. "You should. A hen delicate as you could catch a terrible cold. The cold might turn into bronchitis and the bronchitis might turn into pneumonia."

"Oh," said the Cinnamon Hen. She didn't want pneumonia. "Well, for only three-fifty. I suppose."

But who should come driving by but Mr. Rabbit in his shiny red truck.

"What are you doing that for when I could do it for you?" he asked. "The whole yard. I'll rake it for three-fifty."

"That's quite reasonable," said the Cinnamon Hen.

"And you could go back inside," said Mr. Rabbit. "You shouldn't be out in this cold weather."

The Cinnamon Hen decided she would rake some leaves. She went outside in her old red sweater and black rubber galoshes and began raking the leaves into a pile.

"Oh, Autumn!" she said. "I do enjoy the crunch and scrunch of the leaves."

For Dominic

E
DUTTON
C.4

Atheneum
Macmillan Publishing Company
866 Third Avenue, New York, NY 10022
Collier Macmillan Canada, Inc.

Designed by Barbara A. Fitzsimmons
Text composition by Linoprint Composition, New York, N.Y.
Printed and bound by Toppan Printing Company, Japan

First Edition

10 9 8 7 6 5 4 3 2 1

Library of Congress Cataloging-in-Publication Data

Dutton, Sandra.
The cinnamon hen's autumn day/written and illustrated by Sandra
Dutton.—1st ed.
p.   cm.
Summary: Despite Mr. Rabbit's admonition that raking leaves in the
cool autumn air is bad for her, the Cinnamon Hen finds that she
enjoys that activity too much to give it up.
ISBN 0-689-31414-0
[1. Autumn—Fiction.   2. Chickens—Fiction.   3. Animals—Fiction.]
I. Title.
PZ7.D952Ci 1988
[E]—dc19   87-30290   CIP   AC

The Cinnamon Hen's Autumn Day

written and illustrated by
Sandra Dutton

ATHENEUM   1988   NEW YORK